Tomie dePaola's FAVORITE NURSERY TALES

G·P·Putnam's Sons
New York

For my mother, Flossie Downey dePaola,
whose lap I sat on a long time ago, and
listened to her tell me many of these stories.
TdeP

The Frog Prince, translated by Wanda Gág, reprinted by permission of
Coward-McCann, Inc. from *Tales From Grimm*, translated by Wanda Gág,
copyright © 1936 by Wanda Gág, copyright renewed © 1964 by Robert Janssen.

Illustrations copyright © 1986 by Tomie dePaola. All rights reserved.
Published simultaneously in Canada by General Publishing Co. Limited, Toronto.
Printed in Hong Kong by South China Printing Co. First Impression.
Book design by Nanette Stevenson. Calligraphy by Jeanyee Wong

Library of Congress Cataloging-in-Publication Data dePaola, Tomie. Tomie dePaola's
Favorite nursery tales. Summary: An illustrated collection of poems, fables, and stories
for the nursery, with an emphasis on traditional tales. 1. Tales. 2. Fables. [1. Folklore.
2. Fables] I. Title. PZ8.1.D43TO 1986 398'.8 [E] 85-28302 ISBN 0-399-21319-8

Contents

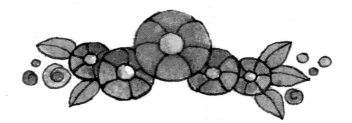

How am I to sing your praise,
Happy chimney-corner days,
Sitting safe in nursery nooks,
Reading picture story-books?

The Children's Hour

by Henry Wadsworth Longfellow

Between the dark and the daylight
    When the night is beginning to lower,
Comes a pause in the day's occupations,
    That is known as the Children's Hour.

I hear in the chamber above me
    The patter of little feet,
The sound of a door that is opened,
    And voices soft and sweet.

From my study I see in the lamplight,
    Decending the broad hall stair,
Grave Alice, and laughing Allegra,
    And Edith with golden hair.

A whisper, and then a silence:
    Yet I know by their merry eyes
They are plotting and planning together
    To take me by surprise.

A sudden rush from the stairway.
    A sudden raid from the hall!
By three doors left unguarded
    They enter my castle wall!

They climb up into my turret
    O'er the arms and back of my chair;
If I try to escape, they surround me;
    They seem to be everywhere.

They almost devour me with kisses,
    Their arms about me entwine,
Till I think of the bishop of Bingen
    In his Mouse-Tower on the Rhine!

Do you think, O blue-eyed banditti,
    Because you have scaled the wall,
Such an old moustache as I am
    Is not a match for you all!

I have you fast in my fortress,
    And will not let you depart,
But put you down into the dungeon
    In the round-tower of my heart.

And there will I keep you forever,
    Yes, forever and a day,
Till the walls shall crumble to ruin,
    And moulder in dust away!

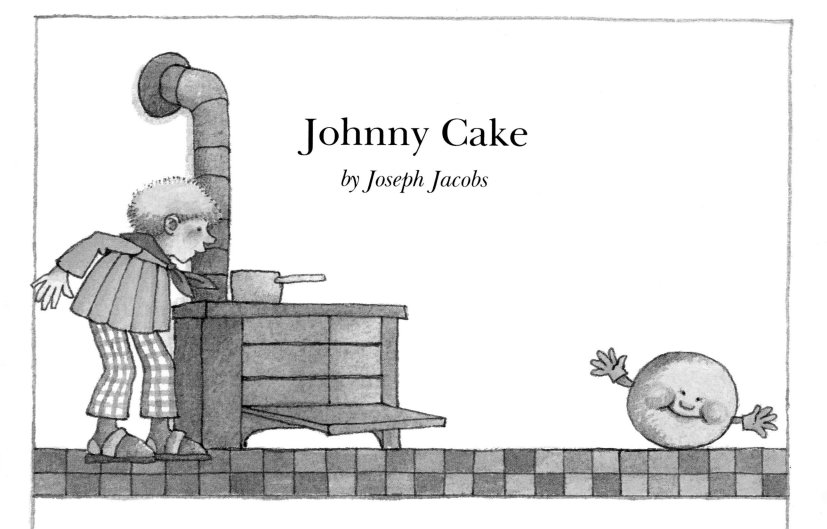

Johnny Cake

by Joseph Jacobs

Once upon a time there was an old man and an old woman and a little boy. One morning the old woman made a Johnny Cake and put it into the oven to bake. "You watch the Johnny Cake while your father and I go out to work in the garden," she told the little boy. And the old man and the old woman went to hoe the potatoes.

But the little boy didn't watch the Johnny Cake all the time. All of a sudden he heard a noise and just as he turned around to see what it was, the oven door popped open and out jumped Johnny Cake and rolled toward the kitchen door.

The little boy ran to shut the door, but Johnny Cake was too quick for him and he was out the door, down the steps, and onto the road before the little boy could catch him. The little boy cried out to his father and mother, who heard the uproar and threw down their hoes and joined the chase. But Johnny Cake outran all three and was out of sight as they sat down, all out of breath, to take a rest.

On went Johnny Cake, and by-and-by he came to two well diggers who looked up from their work and called out, "Where are you going, Johnny Cake?"

"I've outrun an old man and an old woman and a little boy, and I can outrun you too-o-o!"

"You can, can you? We'll see about that!" they said, and they threw down their picks and ran after him. But they couldn't catch up with him and soon they had to sit down exhausted on the side of the road to rest.

On ran Johnny Cake, and by-and-by he came to two ditch diggers who were digging a ditch. "Where are you going, Johnny Cake?" they called out.

"I've outrun an old man and an old woman and a little boy, and two well diggers, and I can outrun you too-o-o!"

"You can, can you? We'll see about that!" they said, and they threw down their spades and ran after him. But Johnny Cake soon outran them too, and seeing that they could never catch up, they gave up and sat down panting, to rest.

On went Johnny Cake, and by-and-by he came to a bear. "Where are you going, Johnny Cake?" the bear asked, licking his lips.

"I've outrun an old man and an old woman and a little boy, and two well diggers, and two ditch diggers, and I can outrun you too-o-o!"

"You can, can you?" growled the bear. "We'll see about that!" And he trotted as fast as his legs could carry him after Johnny Cake, who never even looked back. Before long the bear was so far behind that he gave up and stretched himself out on a grassy bank to rest.

On went Johnny Cake, and by-and-by he came to a wolf. "Where are you going, Johnny Cake?" the wolf called out.

"I've outrun an old man, an old woman, and a little boy, and two well diggers, and two ditch diggers, and a bear, and I can outrun you too-o-o!"

"You can, can you?" snarled the wolf. "We'll see about that!" And he galloped after Johnny Cake who went on and on so fast that the wolf too saw that there was no hope of catching him, and he lay down to rest.

On went Johnny Cake, and by-and-by he came to a fox stretched out quietly by a fence. The fox called out in a sharp voice, "Where are you going, Johnny Cake?" But he didn't get up.

"I've outrun an old man, an old woman, and a little boy, and two well diggers, and two ditch diggers, and a bear, and a wolf, and I can outrun you too-o-o!"

But the fox stayed where he was and said softly, "I can't quite

hear you, Johnny Cake. Won't you come a little closer?" And he turned his head a little to one side.

Johnny Cake stopped running for the first time. He went a little closer to the fox and called out in a very loud voice, "I've outrun an old man, an old woman, and a little boy, and two well diggers, and two ditch diggers, and a bear, and a wolf, and I can outrun you too-o-o!"

"I can't quite hear you. Won't you come just a little closer?" the fox said in a feeble voice as he stretched out his neck toward Johnny Cake and put one paw behind his ear as if to hear better.

Johnny Cake went close, and leaning toward the fox he screamed out, "I've outrun an old man, an old woman and a little boy, and two well diggers, and two ditch diggers, and a bear, and a wolf, and I can outrun you too-o-o!"

"You can, can you!" yelped the fox, and he snapped up the Johnny Cake and gulped him down in the twinkling of an eye.

The Little Red Hen

by Joseph Jacobs

One day the Little Red Hen was scratching in the farm-yard when she found a grain of wheat.

"Who will help plant the wheat?" said she.

"Not I," said the duck.

"Not I," said the cat.

"Not I," said the dog.

"Very well then," said the Little Red Hen, "I will do so myself." So she planted the grain of wheat.

After some time the wheat grew tall and ripe.

"Who will help me cut the wheat?" asked the Little Red Hen.

"Not I," said the duck.

"Not I," said the cat.

"Not I," said the dog.

"Very well then, I will cut it myself," said the Little Red Hen. So she cut the wheat.

"Now," she said, "who will help me thresh the wheat?"

"Not I," said the duck.

"Not I," said the cat.

"Not I," said the dog.

"Very well then, I will thresh it myself," said the Little Red Hen. So she threshed the wheat.

When the wheat was threshed, she said, "Who will help me take the wheat to the mill to have it ground into flour?"

"Not I," said the duck.

"Not I," said the cat.

"Not I," said the dog.

"Very well then, I will take it myself," said the Little Red Hen. So she took the wheat to the mill.

When the wheat was ground into flour, she said, "Who will help me make this flour into bread?"

"Not I," said the duck.

"Not I," said the cat.

"Not I," said the dog.

"Very well then, I will make it myself," said the Little Red Hen, and then she baked a lovely loaf of bread.

Then she said, "Who will help me eat the bread?"

"Oh! I will," said the duck.

"Oh! I will," said the cat.

"Oh, I will," said the dog.

"Oh, no, you won't!" said the Little Red Hen. "I and my chicks will." And she called her chicks and shared the bread with them.

The Frog Prince

by The Brothers Grimm
translated and retold by Wanda Gág

In the olden days when wishing was still of some use, there lived a King. He had several beautiful daughters, but the youngest was so fair that even the sun, who sees so many wonders, could not help marveling every time he looked into her face.

Near the King's palace lay a large dark forest and there, under an old linden tree, was a well. When the day was very warm, the little Princess would go off into this forest and sit at the rim of the cool well. There she would play with her golden ball, tossing it up and catching it deftly in her little hands. This was her favorite game and she never tired of it.

Now it happened one day that, as the Princess tossed her golden ball into the air, it did not fall into her uplifted hands as usual. Instead, it fell to the ground, rolled to the rim of the well and into the water. Plunk, splash! The golden ball was gone.

The well was deep and the Princess knew it. She felt sure she would never see her beautiful ball again, so she cried and cried and could not stop.

"What is the matter, little Princess?" said a voice behind her. "You are crying so that even a hard stone would have pity on you."

The little girl looked around and there she saw a frog. He was in the well and was stretching his fat ugly head out of the water.

"Oh, it's you—you old water-splasher!" said the girl. "I'm crying over my golden ball. It has fallen into the well."

"Oh, as to that," said the frog, "I can bring your ball back to you. But what will you give me if I do?"

"Whatever you wish, dear old frog," said the Princess. "I'll give you my dresses, my beads, and all my jewelry—even the golden crown on my head."

The frog answered: "Your dresses, your beads, and all your jewelry, even the golden crown on your head—I don't want them. But if you can find it in your heart to like me and take me for your playfellow, if you will let me sit beside you at the table, eat from your little golden plate and drink from your little golden cup, and if you are willing to let me sleep in your own little bed besides: if you promise me all this, little Princess, then I will gladly go down to the bottom of the well and bring back your golden ball."

"Oh yes," said the Princess, "I'll promise anything you say if you'll only bring back my golden ball to me." But to herself she thought: "What is the silly frog chattering about? He can only live in the water and croak with the other frogs; he could never be a playmate to a human being."

As soon as the frog had heard her promise, he disappeared into the well. Down, down, down, he sank; but he soon came up again, holding the golden ball in his mouth. He dropped it on the grass

at the feet of the Princess, who was wild with joy when she saw her favorite plaything once more. She picked up the ball and skipped away with it, thinking no more about the little creature who had returned it to her.

"Wait! Wait!" cried the frog. "Take me with you, I can't run as fast as you."

But what good did it do him to scream his "Quark! Quark!" after her as loud as he could? She wouldn't listen to him but hurried home where she soon forgot the poor frog, who now had to go back into his well again.

The next evening, the Princess was eating her dinner at the royal table when—plitch, plotch, plitch, plotch—something came climbing up the stairs. When it reached the door, it knocked at the door and cried:

Youngest daughter of the King,
Open the door for me!

The Princess rose from the table and ran to see who was calling her—when she opened the door, there sat the frog, wet and green and cold! Quickly she slammed the door and sat down at the table again, her heart beating loud and fast. The King could see well enough that she was frightened and worried, and he said,

"My child, what are you afraid of? Is there a giant out there who wants to carry you away?"

"Oh no," said the Princess, "it's not a giant, but a horrid old frog!"

"And what does he want of you?" asked the King.

"Oh, dear Father, as I was playing under the linden tree by the well, my golden ball fell into the water. And because I cried so hard, the frog brought it back to me; and because he insisted so much, I promised him that he could be my playmate. But I never, never thought that he would ever leave his well. Now he is out there and wants to come in and eat from my plate and drink from my cup and sleep in my little bed. But I couldn't bear that, Papa, he's so wet and ugly and his eyes bulge out!"

While she was talking, the frog knocked at the door once more and said:

> *Youngest daughter of the King,*
> *Open the door for me.*
> *Mind your words at the old well spring;*
> *Open the door for me!*

At that the King said, "If we make promises, daughter, we must keep them; so you had better go and open the door."

The Princess still did not want to do it but she had to obey. When she opened the door, the frog hopped in and followed her until she reached her chair. Then he sat there and said, "Lift me up beside you."

She hesitated—the frog was so cold and clammy—but her father looked at her sternly and said, "You must keep your promise."

After the frog was on her chair, he wanted to be put on the table. When he was there, he said, "Now shove your plate a little closer, so we can eat together like real playmates."

The Princess shuddered, but she had to do it. The frog enjoyed the meal and ate heartily, but the poor girl could not swallow a single bite. At last the frog said, "Now I've eaten enough and I feel tired. Carry me to your room so I can go to sleep."

The Princess began to cry. It had been hard enough to touch the cold, fat frog, and worse still to have him eat out of her plate, but to have him beside her in her little bed was more than she could bear.

"I want to go to bed," repeated the frog. "Take me there and tuck me in."

The Princess shuddered again and looked at her father, but he only said, "He helped you in your trouble. Is it fair to scorn him now?"

There was nothing for her to do but to pick up the creature—she did it with two fingers—and to carry him up into her room,

where she dropped him in a corner on the floor, hoping he would be satisfied. But after she had gone to bed, she heard something she didn't like. Ploppety plop! Ploppety plop! It was the frog hopping across the room, and when he reached her bed he said, "I'm tired and the floor is too hard. I have as much right as you to sleep in a good soft bed. Lift me up or I will tell your father."

At this the Princess was bitterly angry, but she picked him up and put him at the foot-end of her bed. There he stayed all night,

but when the dark was graying into daylight, the frog jumped down from the bed, out of the door and away, she knew not where.

The next night it was the same. The frog came back, knocked at the door and said:

> *Youngest daughter of the King,*
> *Open the door for me.*
> *Mind your words at the old well spring;*
> *Open the door for me!*

There was nothing for her to do but let him in. Again he ate out of her golden plate, sipped out of her golden cup, and again he slept at the foot-end of her bed. In the morning, he went away as before.

The third night he came again. This time he was not content to sleep at her feet.

"I want to sleep under your pillow," he said. "I think I'd like it better there."

The girl thought she would never be able to sleep with a horrid, damp, goggle-eyed frog under her pillow. She began to weep softly to herself and couldn't stop until at last she cried herself to sleep.

When the night was over and the morning sunlight burst in at the window, the frog crept out from under her pillow and hopped off the bed. But as soon as his feet touched the floor, something happened to him. In that moment he was no longer a cold, fat, goggle-eyed frog, but a young Prince with handsome friendly eyes!

"You see," he said, "I wasn't what I seemed to be! A wicked old woman bewitched me. No one but you could break the spell, little Princess, and I waited and waited at the well for you to help me."

The Princess was speechless with surprise but her eyes sparkled.

"And will you let me be your playmate now?" said the Prince, laughing. "Mind your words at the old well spring!"

At this the Princess laughed too, and they both ran out to play with the golden ball.

For years they were the best of friends and the happiest of playmates, and it is not hard to guess, I'm sure, that when they were grown-up they were married and lived happily ever after.

The Lion and the Mouse

by Aesop

Once there was a mouse who happened to run into a lion who caught the mouse and was just about to eat him when the mouse begged the lion to let him go. "Please, if you let me go, I shall be forever grateful."

The mouse was so small and pitiful that the lion laughed when he thought what a tiny mouthful the mouse would be. And so the lion let the mouse go.

Not long after, the lion was caught in a net made of strong rope that some hunters had put out. He roared and roared and guess who heard him? The mouse! "Well, Mr. Lion," the mouse said, "when you laughed at how small I was, I guess you had no idea that someday I could help you." And with that the mouse gnawed through the rope and set the lion free.

Moral: Sometimes the most powerful owe everything to the smallest and weakest.

The Three Little Pigs

by Joseph Jacobs

Long ago there lived a mother pig who had three little pigs. The mother pig was very poor, and at last she had to send her pigs out to seek their fortunes.

The first little pig that went away met a man with a bundle of straw, and he said to him, "Please, man, give me that straw so I can build me a house."

The man gave the straw to the little pig. Then the pig built a house of the straw and lived in the house.

By and by a wolf came along and knocked at the door of the little straw house.

"Little pig, little pig, let me come in!" called the wolf.

"No, not by the hair of my chinny, chin chin, I'll not let you in," answered the pig.

"Then I'll huff and I'll puff and I'll blow your house in," said the wolf.

So he huffed and he puffed and he blew the house in. Then he chased the little pig away.

The second little pig that went away met a man with a bundle of sticks, and he said to the man, "Please, man, give me your bundle of sticks so I can build me a house." The man gave the sticks to the little pig. Then the pig built a house of the sticks and lived in the house. By and by the wolf came along and knocked at the door of the little house of sticks.

"Little pig, little pig, let me come in!" called the wolf.

"No, not by the hair of my chinny, chin, chin, I'll not let you in," answered the pig.

"Then I'll huff and I'll puff and I'll blow your house in," said the wolf.

So he huffed and he puffed and he blew the house in. Then he chased the little pig away.

The third pig that went away met a man with a load of bricks, and he said, "Please, man, give me your load of bricks so I can build me a house." The man gave the bricks to the little pig. Then the pig built a house with the bricks and lived in the house.

At last the wolf came along and knocked at the door of the brick house.

"Little pig, little pig, let me come in!" called the wolf.

"No, not by the hair of my chinny, chin, chin, I'll not let you in," answered the pig.

"Then I'll huff and I'll puff and I'll blow your house in," said the wolf.

So he huffed and he puffed and he puffed and he huffed, but he could not blow the little brick house in.

The wolf rested a few minutes, and then he said, "Little pig, little pig, will you let just the tip of my nose in?"

"No," said the little pig.

"Little pig, little pig, will you let just my paw in?"

"No," said the little pig.

"Little pig, little pig, will you let just the tip of my tail in?"

No," said the little pig.

"Then I will climb up on the roof and come down through the chimney," said the wolf.

But the little pig made the fire very hot, so the wolf could not come down the chimney. So he went away, and that was the end of him.

The little pig then went and fetched his mother, and they still live happily in their little brick house.

My Shadow

by Robert Louis Stevenson

I have a little shadow that goes in and out with me,
And what can be the use of him is more than I can see.
He is very, very like me from the heels up to the head;
And I see him jump before me, when I jump into my bed.

The funniest thing about him is the way he likes to grow—
Not at all like proper children, which is always very slow;
For he sometimes shoots up taller like an india-rubber ball,
And he sometimes gets so little that there's none of him at all.

He hasn't got a notion of how children ought to play,
And can only make a fool of me in every sort of way.
He stays so close beside me, he's a coward you can see;
I'd think shame to stick to nursie as that shadow sticks to me!

One morning very early, before the sun was up,
I rose and found the shining dew on every buttercup;
But my lazy little shadow, like an arrant sleepyhead,
Had stayed at home behind me and was fast asleep in bed.

The Three Billy-Goats Gruff

by P. C. Asbjörnsen

Once upon a time there were three billy-goats, who wanted to go up to the hillside to make themselves fat, and the name of all three was Gruff.

On the way up was a bridge over a mountain stream they had to cross; and under the bridge lived a great ugly Troll, with eyes as big as saucers, and a nose as long as a poker.

The first to cross the bridge was the youngest billy-goat Gruff.

"Trip, trap; trip, trap!" went the bridge.

"Who's that tripping over my bridge?" roared the Troll.

"Oh! It is only I, the tiniest billy-goat Gruff; and I'm going up to the hillside to make myself fat," said the billy-goat with such a small voice.

"Well, I'm coming to gobble you up," said the Troll.

"Oh, no! Please don't gobble me up. I'm too little, that I am," said the billy-goat. "Wait a bit till the second billy-goat Gruff comes. He's much bigger."

"Well! Be off with you," said the Troll.

A little while later the second billy-goat Gruff came to cross the bridge.

"Trip, trap! Trip, trap! Trip trap!" went the bridge.

"Who's that tripping over my bridge?" roared the Troll.

"Oh! It's I, the second billy-goat Gruff, and I'm going up to the hillside to make myself fat," said the billy-goat, who hadn't such a small voice.

"Well, I'm coming to gobble you up," said the Troll.

"Oh, no! Please don't gobble me up. Wait a little till the big billy-goat Gruff comes. He's much bigger."

"Very well! Be off with you," said the Troll.

But just then up came the big billy-goat Gruff.

"Trip, trap! Trip, trap! Trip, trap!" went the bridge, for the billy-goat was so heavy that the bridge creaked and groaned under him.

"*Who's that* tramping over my bridge?" roared the Troll.

"*It's I! The big billy-goat Gruff,*" said the billy-goat, who had an ugly, hoarse voice of his own.

"Well, I'm coming to gobble you up," roared the Troll.

"Well, come along! I've got two spears,
And I'll poke your nose and pierce your ears;
I've got besides two curling-stones,
And I'll bruise your body and rattle your bones."

That was what the big billy-goat said; and then he flew at the Troll and tossed him into the water. And the third billy-goat Gruff went up to the hillside. There the billy-goats got so fat they were scarcely able to walk home again; and if the fat hasn't fallen off them, why they're still fat, and so:

Snip, snap, snout,
This tale's told out.

Rumpelstiltskin

by The Brothers Grimm

There was once a miller who was very poor, but he had a beautiful daughter. Now it once happened that he had occasion to speak with the King, and in order to give himself an air of importance he said, "I have a daughter who can spin gold out of straw."

The King said to the miller, "That is an art in which I am much interested. If your daughter is as skillful as you say she is, bring her to my castle tomorrow, and I will put her to the test."

Accordingly, when the maiden was brought to the castle, the King conducted her to a chamber which was quite full of straw, gave her a spinning wheel and a reel, and said, "Now set to work. And if between tonight and tomorrow at dawn you have not spun this straw into gold, you must die." Thereupon he carefully locked the door of the chamber, and she remained alone. There sat the unfortunate miller's daughter, and for the life of her she did not know what to do. She had not the least idea how to spin straw into gold, and she became more and more distressed until at last she began to weep. Then all at once the door sprang open, and in stepped a little man who said, "Good evening, Mistress Miller. What are you weeping so for?"

"Alas," answered the maiden, "I've got to spin gold out of straw and don't know how to do it."

Then the little man said, "What will you give me if I spin it for you?"

"My necklace," said the maid.

The little man took the necklace, sat down before the spinning wheel, and whir—whir—whir, in a trice the reel was full. Then he fixed another reel, and whir—whir—whir, thrice round, and that too was full. And so it went on until morning, when all the straw was spun and all the reels were full of gold.

Immediately at sunrise the King came, and when he saw the gold he was astonished and much pleased, but his mind became only the more greedy. So he had the miller's daughter taken to another chamber full of straw, larger than the former one, and he ordered her to spin it also in one night, if she valued her life.

The maiden was at her wit's end and began to weep. Then again the door sprang open, and the little man appeared and said,

"What will you give me if I spin the straw into gold for you?"

"The ring off my finger," answered the maiden.

The little man took the ring, began to whir again at the wheel, and by morning had spun all the straw into gold.

The King was delighted at the sight of the masses of gold, but he was not even yet satisfied. So he had the miller's daughter taken to a still larger chamber full of straw and said, "This must you spin tonight into gold, but if you succeed you shall become my Queen." "Even if she is only a miller's daughter," thought he, "I shan't find a richer woman in the whole world."

When the girl was alone the little man came again and said for the third time, "What will you give me if I spin the straw for you this time?"

"I have nothing more to give," answered the girl.

"Well, promise me your first child if you become Queen."

"Who knows what may happen?" thought the miller's daughter, but she did not see any other way of getting out of the difficulty. So she promised the little man what he demanded, and in return he spun the straw into gold once more.

When the King came in the morning and found everything as he had wished, he celebrated his marriage with her, and the miller's daughter became Queen.

About a year afterwards a beautiful child was born, but the Queen had forgotten all about the little man. However, he suddenly entered her chamber and said, "Now, give me what you promised."

The Queen was terrified, and she offered the little man all the wealth of the kingdom if he would let her keep the child. But the little man said, "No, I would rather have some living thing than all the treasures of the world."

Then the Queen began to moan and weep to such an extent that the little man felt sorry for her. "I will give you three days," said he, "and if within that time you discover my name you shall keep the child."

Then during the night the Queen called to mind all the names that she had ever heard, and she sent a messenger all over the country to inquire far and wide what other names there were.

When the little man appeared the next day, she began with Caspar, Melchior, Balthazar, and mentioned all the names which she knew, one after the other. But at every one the little man said, "No. No. That's not my name."

The second day she had inquiries made all round the neighborhood for the names of people living there and suggested to the little man all the most unusual and strange names. "Perhaps your name is Cowribs, or Spindleshanks, or Spiderlegs?"

But again he answered, "No. That's not my name."

On the third day the messenger came back and said, "I haven't been able to find any new names, but as I came round the corner of a wood on a lofty mountain, where the fox says good night to the hare, I saw a little house, and in front of the house a fire was burning. And around the fire a most ridiculous little man was leaping. He was hopping on one leg and singing:

> *Today I bake; tomorrow I brew my beer;*
> *The next day I will bring the Queen's child here.*
> *Ah, lucky 'tis that not a soul doth know*
> *That Rumpelstiltskin is my name. Ho! Ho!*

You can imagine how delighted the Queen was when she heard the name! And soon afterwards, when the little man came in and asked, "Now, Your Majesty, what is my name?" at first she asked, "Is your name Tom?"

"No."

"Is it Dick?"

"No."

"Is it, by chance, Rumpelstiltskin?"

"The devil told you that! The devil told you that!" shrieked the little man. And in his rage he stamped his right foot into the ground so deep that he sank up to his waist.

Then he seized his left leg in one hand and his right leg in the other and pulled. And that was the end of Rumpelstiltskin.

The Country Maid and Her Milkpail

by Aesop

Once a country maid was walking slowly along with a pail of milk on her head. As she began to think about what she was going to do with the milk, she said to herself, "With the money I get for selling this milk, I can buy three hundred eggs. These eggs will produce at least two hundred fifty chickens. The chickens will grow, and at Christmas they will be fine fat birds and bring a good price. Then I shall have money to buy a new dress— a green one because the color suits me best. In this dress I shall go to the fair. At the fair, all the young men will want to dance with me, but I shall refuse everyone because I shall look so fancy." At this she stuck her nose up in the air, forgetting all about the pail of milk she carried on her head. Over it went and all the milk spilled onto the ground.

Moral: Don't count your chickens before they hatch.

The Three Bears

by Joseph Jacobs

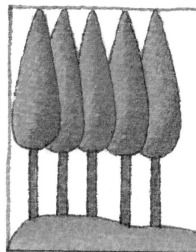

Once upon a time there were Three Bears who lived together in a house in a wood. One of them was a Small Wee Bear; one was a Middle-Sized Bear; and the last was a Great Huge Bear. They each had a pot for their porridge: a small pot for the Small Wee Bear; a middle-sized pot for the Middle-Sized Bear; and a great huge pot for the Great Huge Bear. And they each had a chair to sit in: a small chair for the Small Wee Bear; a middle-sized chair for the Middle-Sized Bear; and a great huge chair for the Great Huge Bear. And they each had a bed to sleep in: a small bed for the Small Wee Bear; a middle-sized one for the Middle-Sized Bear; and a great huge bed for the Great Huge Bear.

One day, after they had made their breakfast porridge and poured it into their porridge pots, they went for a walk in the wood, leaving the porridge to cool so that they wouldn't burn their mouths by eating it too soon.

While they were out walking, a little girl came into the clearing where their house was. She could not have been a good little girl because she peeped into the window and then peered through the keyhole to see if anyone was home. And seeing nobody in the house, she lifted the latch and went in.

Inside the house, the little girl saw the porridge pots on the table. If she had been a good little girl she would have waited till the Bears came home, and then perhaps they would have asked her to have breakfast with them. But she was a naughty little girl so she set about helping herself. First she tasted the porridge of the Great Huge Bear but it was too hot for her. (And she said a bad word about that.)

Then she tasted the porridge of the Middle-Sized Bear and that was too cold for her. (And she said a bad word about that too.)

And then she found the porridge of the Small Wee Bear and tasted that. It was neither too hot nor too cold, but just right. And she liked it so much that she ate it all up. (But the naughty little girl even said a bad word about that little pot because it did not hold enough porridge for her.)

Then the little girl sat down in the chair of the Great Huge Bear. But that was too hard for her. Next she sat down in the chair of the Middle-Sized Bear but that was too soft for her. And then she sat down in the chair of the Small Wee Bear and that was neither too hard, nor too soft, but just right. So she sat and sat until the bottom fell out and down she went, bump onto the floor. (And the little girl said a bad word about that too.)

Then the little girl went upstairs and into the bedroom where the Three Bears slept. First she lay down on the bed of the Huge Great Bear but the pillow was too high. Next she lay down on the bed of the Middle-Sized Bear but the pillow was too flat. Then she lay down on the bed of the Small Wee Bear and the pillow was neither too high, nor too flat, but just right. So she covered herself up and was so comfortable that she fell fast asleep.

By this time, the Three Bears thought their porridge would be cool enough to eat, so they went home for breakfast. Now the little girl had left the spoon of the Great Huge Bear standing in his porridge. "Somebody has been eating my porridge!" said the Great Huge Bear in his great rough gruff voice.

And when the Middle-Sized Bear looked at his porridge, he saw that the spoon was standing in it too.

"Somebody has been eating my porridge!" said the Middle-Sized Bear in his middle voice.

Then the Small Wee Bear looked at his, and the spoon was in the porridge pot but the porridge was all gone.

"Somebody has been eating my porridge and has eaten it all up!" said the Small Wee Bear in his small wee voice.

The Three Bears, seeing that someone had come into their house and eaten up the Small Wee Bear's breakfast, began to look for whoever it was. Now the little girl had not put the hard cushion straight when she got up from the chair of the Great Huge Bear.

"Somebody has been sitting in my chair!" said the Great Huge Bear in his great rough gruff voice.

And the little girl had pressed down the soft cushion of the Middle-Sized Bear.

"Somebody has been sitting in my chair!" said the Middle-Sized Bear in his middle voice.

And you know what the little girl had done to the third chair.

"Somebody has been sitting in my chair and has sat the bottom out of it!" said the Small Wee Bear in his small wee voice.

Then the Three Bears thought they had better look upstairs. So they went up to their bedroom.

Now the little girl had pulled the pillow of the Great Huge Bear off the bed. "Somebody has been lying in my bed!" said the Great Huge Bear in his great rough gruff voice.

And the little girl had left the pillow of the Middle-Sized Bear at the foot of the bed.

"Somebody has been lying in my bed!" said the Middle-Sized Bear in his middle voice.

And when the Small Wee Bear looked at his bed, the pillow was in its right place, but on the pillow was the head of the little girl, which was not in the right place, for she should not have been there at all! "Somebody has been lying in my bed, and here she is!" said the Small Wee Bear in his small wee voice.

Even though she was fast asleep, the little girl had heard the great rough gruff voice of the Great Huge Bear as if in a dream. And she had heard the middle voice of the Middle-Sized Bear, but she still didn't wake up. But when she heard the small wee voice of the Small Wee Bear, it was so sharp and shrill and close that it woke her up at once.

Up she started and when she saw the Three Bears looking at her from one side of the bed, she tumbled out of the other side and ran to the window which was open. Out jumped the little girl, and whether she hurt herself when she hit the ground, or found her way home through the wood, or was punished for staying away from school that day no one knows. But she was never seen by the Three Bears again.

Belling the Cat

by Aesop

Once there was a cat who was such a good mouser that all the mice in the house were terrified. The mice decided to call a meeting to see if they could figure out a way to keep from being surprised by this sly cat.

"I have an idea," said one of the mice. "If we hang a bell around the cat's neck, we'll be able to hear Kitty as she comes near and we can run and hide."

All the mice agreed that this was a wonderful idea. So they got a bell and a ribbon.

"Now," said another mouse, "who will put the bell around Kitty's neck?"

"Not I," said the mouse whose idea it had been.

"Nor I," said another.

"Or I," said several all at once.

No one was brave enough to bell the cat.

Moral: A good idea is one thing, carrying it out is another.

The Dog and His Shadow

by Aesop

Once a dog was given a nice bone. He put it in his mouth and set off for home. As he was crossing the bridge over a river he looked down and saw his reflection in the water. "Why, there is a dog looking up at me," he said, "and he has a bone too! But his bone is bigger than mine. I'll just drop this smaller bone and grab that bigger bone away."

At that, the dog dropped the bone and jumped into the river, losing the bone for good—and getting very wet as well!

Moral: It's better to be content with what you already have instead of chasing after what's not there.

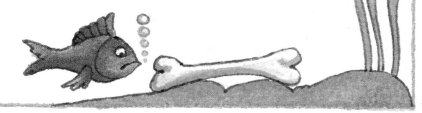

The Princess and the Pea

by Hans Christian Andersen

Once upon a time there was a Prince and he wanted a Princess; but she would have to be a *real* princess. He traveled all around the world to find one, but always there was something wrong. There were Princesses enough, but he found it difficult to make out whether they were *real* ones. There was always something about them that was not quite right. So he came home again and was very sad, for he would have liked very much to have a real Princess.

One evening a terrible storm came on; it thundered and lightened, and the rain poured down in torrents. It was really dreadful! Suddenly a knocking was heard at the city gate, and the old King himself went to open it.

It was a Princess standing out there before the gate. But good gracious! What a sight she was after all the rain and the dreadful weather! The water ran down from her hair and her clothes; it ran down into the toes of her shoes and out again at the heels. And yet she said that she was a real Princess.

"Yes, we'll soon find that out," thought the old Queen. But she said nothing, went into the bedroom, took all the bedding off the bedstead, and laid a pea at the bottom; then she took twenty mattresses and laid them on the pea, and then twenty eiderdown beds on top of the mattresses.

On this the Princess was to lie all night. In the morning she was asked how she had slept.

"Oh, terribly badly!" said the Princess. "I have scarcely shut my eyes the whole night. Heaven only knows what was in the bed, but I was lying on something hard, so that I am black and blue all over my body. It is really terrible."

Now they knew that she was a real Princess, because she had felt the pea right through the twenty mattresses and the twenty eiderdown beds.

Nobody but a real Princess could be as sensitive as that.

So the Prince took her for his wife, for now he knew that he had a real Princess; and the pea was put in the Art Museum, where it may still be seen, if no one has stolen it.

There, that is a *real* story!

The Owl and the Pussycat

by Edward Lear

The Owl and the Pussycat went to sea
    In a beautiful pea-green boat:
They took some honey, and plenty of money
    Wrapped up in a five-pound note.

The Owl looked up to the stars above,
    And sang to a small guitar,
"O lovely Pussy! O Pussy, my love,
    What a beautiful Pussy you are,
You are, you are!
    What a beautiful Pussy you are!"

Pussy said to the Owl, "You elegant fowl!
    How charmingly sweet you sing!
O let us be married! too long we have tarried:
    But what shall we do for a ring?"

They sailed away for a year and a day,
    To the land where the Bong tree grows,
And there in a wood a Piggy-wig stood,
    With a ring at the end of his nose,
His nose, his nose,
    With a ring at the end of his nose.

"Dear Pig, are you willing to sell for one shilling
    Your ring?" Said the Piggy, "I will."
So they took it away, and were married next day
    By the Turkey who lives on the hill.

They dined on mince, and slices of quince,
    Which they ate with a runcible spoon;
And hand in hand, on the edge of the sand,
    They danced by the light of the moon,
The moon, the moon,
    They danced by the light of the moon.

Johnny and the Three Goats

from the Norwegian

Every morning Johnny drove his three goats to the pasture and every evening when the sun was going to bed he brought them home again.

One morning he set off early, driving the goats before him and whistling as he trudged along.

Just as he reached Mr. Smith's turnip field what should he see but a broken board in the fence.

The goats saw it too, and in they skipped and began running round and round, stopping now and then to nip off the tops of the tender young turnips.

Johnny knew that would never do.

Picking up a stick, he climbed through the fence and tried to drive the goats out.

But never were there such naughty goats.

Round and round they went, not once going toward the hole in the fence.

Johnny ran and ran and ran till he could run no more, and then he crawled through the hole in the fence and sat down beside the road and began to cry.

Just then who should come
down the road but the fox.

"Good morning, Johnny!" said
he. "What are you crying about?"

"I'm crying because I can't get the
goats out of the turnip field," said Johnny.

"Oh, don't cry about that," said the fox. "I'll
drive them out for you." So over the fence leapt the fox,
and round and round the turnip field he ran after the goats.
But no, they would not go out.

They flicked their tails and shook their heads and away they
went, trampling down the turnips until you could hardly have
told what had been growing in the field.

The fox ran till he could run no more. Then he went over and
sat down beside Johnny, and he began to cry.

Down the road came a rabbit.
"Good morning, Fox," he said.
"What are you crying about?"
"I'm crying because Johnny is
crying," said the fox, "and Johnny
is crying because he can't get the goats out of the turnip field."
"Tut, tut!" said the rabbit. "What a thing to cry about! Watch me.
I'll soon drive them out."
The rabbit hopped over the fence.
Round and round the field he chased the goats; but they would
not go near the hole in the fence.
At last the rabbit was so tired he could not hop another hop.

He too crawled through the fence, sat down beside the fox, and began to cry.

Just then a bee came buzzing along over the tops of the flowers.

When she saw the rabbit she said. "Good morning, Bunny, what are you crying about?"

"I'm crying because the fox is crying," said the rabbit, "and the fox is crying because Johnny is crying, and Johnny is crying because he can't get the goats out of the turnip field."

"Don't cry about that," said the bee, "I'll soon get them out for you."

"You!" said the rabbit. "A little thing like you drive the goats out, when neither Johnny, nor the fox, nor I can get them out?" And he laughed at the very idea of such a thing.

"Watch me," said the bee.

Over the fence she flew and she went buzz-z-z right in the ear of the biggest goat.

The goat shook his head and tried to brush away the bee, but the bee only flew to the other ear and she went buzz-z-z there too, until the goat thought there must be some dreadful thing in the turnip field, so out through the hole in the fence he went, and ran down the road to his pasture.

The bee flew over to the second goat and first went buzz-z-z in one ear and then went buzz-z-z in the other, until that goat was willing to follow the other through the fence and down the road to the pasture.

The bee flew after the third goat and buzzed first in one ear and then in the other until he too was glad to follow the others.

"Thank you, little bee," said the rabbit, and he hopped away.

"Thank you, little bee," said the fox, and he ran away.

"Thank you, little bee," said Johnny, and wiping away his tears, he hurried down the road to put the goats in the pasture.

The Straw Ox

from the Russian

Once upon a time there was an old man and an old woman. The old man worked in the field, while the old woman sat at home and spun flax. They were so poor that they could save nothing at all; all their earnings went for black bread, and when that was gone there was nothing left. At last the old woman had a good idea.

"Husband," she cried, "make me a straw ox, and smear it all over with tar."

"Why, you foolish woman!" he said. "What's the good of such an ox?"

"Never mind," she said, "you just make it. I know what I am about."

What was the poor man to do?

He set to work and made the ox of straw and smeared it all over with tar.

The night passed away, and at early dawn the old woman took her distaff and drove the straw ox out to graze, and she herself sat

down behind a hillock and began spinning her flax, and cried:

"Graze away, little ox, while I spin my flax; graze away little ox, while I spin my flax!" And while she spun, her head drooped down, and she began to doze, and while she was dozing, from behind the dark wood and from the back of the huge pines a bear came rushing out upon the ox and said:

"Who are you? Speak and tell me!"

And the ox said:

"A three-year-old heifer am I, made of straw and smeared with tar."

"Oh!" said the bear. "Stuffed with straw and trimmed with tar, are you? Then give me some of your straw and tar, that I may patch up my ragged fur!"

"Take some," said the ox, and the bear fell upon it and began to tear away at the tar.

He tore and tore and buried his teeth in it until he found he couldn't let go again. He tugged and he tugged, but it was no good, and the ox dragged him gradually off, goodness knows where.

Then the old woman awoke, and there was no ox to be seen. "Alas! Old fool that I am!" cried she. "Perchance it has gone home."

Then she quickly caught up her distaff and spinning-board, threw them over her shoulders, and hastened off home, and she saw that the ox had dragged the bear up to the fence, and in she went to her old man. "Husband!" she cried. "Look, look! The ox has brought us a bear. Come out and kill it!"

Then the old man jumped up, tore the bear off the straw ox, tied him up, and threw him in the cellar.

Next morning, between dark and dawn, the old woman took her distaff and drove the ox into the meadow to graze. She herself sat down by a mound, began spinning, and said:

"Graze, graze away, little ox, while I spin my flax! Graze, graze away, little ox, while I spin my flax!" And while she spun, her head drooped down, and she dozed. And, lo! From behind the dark wood, from the back of the huge pines, a gray wolf came rushing out upon the ox and said:
"Who are you? Come, tell me!"

"I am a three-year-old
heifer, stuffed with straw and
trimmed with tar," said the ox.
"Oh, trimmed with tar, are you?
Then give me some of your tar to tar
my sides, so that the dogs will not bite me."
"Take some," said the ox. And with that the wolf fell upon it
and tried to tear the tar off. He tugged and tugged and tore with
his teeth, but he could get none off. Then he tried to let go, and
couldn't; tug and pull as he might, it was no good.

When the old woman woke, there was no ox in sight. "Maybe
my ox has gone home!" she cried. "I'll go home and see."

When she got there she was astonished, for by the paling stood
the ox with the wolf still tugging at it. She ran and told her old
man, and her old man came and threw the wolf into the cellar
also.

On the third day the woman again drove her ox into the pas-
tures to graze, sat down by a mound, and dozed off.

Then a fox came running up.
"Who are you?" she asked the ox.

"I'm a three-year-old heifer,
stuffed with straw and
daubed with tar."

"Then give me some of your tar to smear on my sides, so the dogs won't tear my hide!"

"Take some," said the ox. Then the fox fastened her teeth in it and couldn't draw them out again. The old woman told her old man, and he took and cast the fox into the cellar in the same way. And after that they caught a hare the same way.

So when the old man had them all safely in the cellar, he sat down on a bench before the cellar and began sharpening a knife. And the bear said to him from the cellar window:

"Tell me, Daddy, why are you sharpening your knife?"

"To skin you, that I may make a leather jacket for myself and a vest for my old woman."

"Oh, don't skin me, Daddy dear! Rather, let me go, and I'll bring you a lot of honey."

"Very well, see that you do it." And he untied the bear and let him go. Then he sat down on the bench and again began sharpening his knife. And the wolf asked him:

"Daddy, why are you sharpening your knife?"

"To skin you, that I may make me a warm cap for the winter."

"Oh! Don't skin me, Daddy dear, and I'll bring you a whole herd of little sheep."

"Well, see that you do it." And he let the wolf go.

Then he sat down and began sharpening his knife again.

The fox put out her little snout and asked him:

"Be so kind, dear Daddy, and tell me why you are sharpening your knife?"

"Little foxes," said the old man, "have nice skins that make fine collars and trimmings, and I want to skin you!"

"Oh! Don't take my skin away, Daddy dear, and I will bring you hens and geese."

"Very well, see that you do it!" And he let the fox go.

Now only the hare remained, and the old man began sharpening his knife again.

"Why do you do that?" asked the hare, and the old man replied:

"Little hares have nice little soft warm skins, which will make me nice gloves and mittens against the winter!"

"Oh, Daddy dear! Don't skin me, and I'll bring you kale and good cauliflower, if only you let me go!"

So the old man let the hare go also.

Then the old man and the old woman went to bed, but very early in the morning, when it was neither dusk nor dawn, there was a noise at the door.

"Husband!" cried the old woman. "There's someone scratching at the door; go and see who it is!"

The old man went out, and there was the bear carrying a whole hive full of honey. The old man took the honey from the bear.

No sooner did he lie down than again there was another noise at the door. The old man looked out and saw the wolf driving a whole flock of sheep into the courtyard. Close on his heels came the fox, driving before her geese and hens, and all manner of fowl; and last of all came the hare, bringing cauliflower and kale, and all manner of good food.

And the old man was glad, and the old woman was glad. And the old man sold the sheep and fowl and got so rich that he and the old woman needed nothing more.

As for the straw-stuffed ox, it stood in the sun till it fell to pieces.

The Fox and the Stork

by Aesop

Once a fox invited a stork for dinner. The fox placed a shallow dish on the table and filled it with food. But it was impossible for the stork with her long beak to eat anything, while the fox lapped up everything in the dish with his tongue. How the fox laughed at the poor hungry stork.

Now it was the stork's turn to invite the fox to dine with her. She placed a long-necked jar on the table and filled it with food. The stork had no trouble at all reaching down with her long beak and getting all she wanted, while the fox could get nothing. That night it was the fox who went hungry!

Moral: If you have been rude, don't be surprised if you get paid back.

Master of All Masters

by Joseph Jacobs

A girl once went to the fair to look for work. At last a funny-looking old gentleman hired her and took her home to his house. When she got there, he told her that he had something to teach her, for that in his house he had his own names for things.

He said to her: "What will you call me?"

"Master or mister, or whatever you please, sir," said she.

"You must call me 'master of all masters.' And what would you call this?" he said, pointing to his bed.

"Bed or couch, or whatever you please, sir."

"No, that's my 'barnacle.' And what do you call these?" said he, pointing to his pantaloons.

"Breeches or trousers, or whatever you please, sir."

"You must call them 'squibs and crackers.' And what would you call her?" he asked, pointing to the cat.

"Cat or kit, or whatever you please, sir."

"You must call her 'white-faced simminy.' And this now," showing her the fire, "what would you call this?"

"Fire or flame, or whatever you please, sir."

"You must call it 'hot cockalorum.' And what is this?" he went on, pointing to the water.

"Water or wet, or whatever you please, sir."

"No, 'pondalorum' is its name. And what do you call all this?" asked he, as he pointed to the house.

"House or cottage, or whatever you please, sir."

"You must call it 'high topper mountain.'"

That very night the servant woke her master up in a fright and said: "Master of all masters, get out of your barnacle and put on your squibs and crackers. For white-faced simminy has got a spark of hot cockalorum on its tail, and unless you get some pondalorum, high topper moutain will be all on hot cockalorum."

. . . . That's all.

The Emperor's New Clothes

by Hans Christian Andersen

Many years ago there was an emperor who was so excessively fond of new clothes that he spent all his money upon them. He cared nothing about his soldiers, nor for the theater, nor for driving in the woods except for the sake of showing off his new clothes. He had a costume for every hour in the day, and instead of saying, as one does about any other king or emperor, "He is in his council chamber," here one always said, "The emperor is in his dressing-room."

Life was very gay in the great town where he lived; hosts of strangers came to visit it every day, and among them one day two swindlers. They gave themselves out as weavers and said that they knew how to weave the most beautiful stuffs imaginable. Not only were the colors and patterns unusually fine, but the clothes that were made of the stuffs had the peculiar quality of becoming invisible to every person who was not fit for the office he held, or if he was impossibly dull.

"Those must be splendid clothes," thought the emperor. "By wearing them I should be able to discover which men in my kingdom are unfitted for their posts. I shall distinguish the wise men from the fools. Yes, I certainly must order some of that stuff to be woven for me."

He paid the two swindlers a lot of money in advance so that they might begin their work at once.

They did put up two looms and pretended to weave, but they had nothing whatever upon their shuttles. At the outset they asked for a quantity of the finest silk and the purest gold thread, all of which they put into their own bags while they worked away at the empty looms far into the night.

"I should like to know how those weavers are getting on with the stuff," thought the emperor; but he felt a little queer when he reflected that anyone who was stupid or unfit for his post would not be able to see it. He certainly thought that he need have no fears for himself, but still he thought he would send somebody else first to see how it was getting on. Everybody in the town knew what wonderful power the stuff possessed, and everyone was anxious to see how stupid his neighbor was.

"I will send my faithful old minister to the weavers," thought the emperor. "He will be best able to see how the stuff looks, for he is a clever man and no one fulfills his duties better than he does."

So the good old minister went into the room where the two swindlers sat working at the empty loom.

"Heaven preserve us!" thought the old minister, opening his eyes very wide. "Why, I can't see a thing!" But he took care not to say so.

Both the swindlers begged him to be good enough to step a little nearer and asked if he did not think it a good pattern and beautiful coloring. They pointed to the empty loom, and the poor old minister stared as hard as he could but he could not see anything, for of course there was nothing to see.

"Good Heavens!" thought he. "Is it possible that I am a fool? I have never thought so and nobody must know it. Am I not fit for my post? It will never do to say that I cannot see the stuff."

"Well, sir, you don't say anything about the stuff," said the one who was pretending to weave.

"Oh, it is beautiful! Quite charming!" said the old minister looking through his spectacles. "This pattern and these colors! I will certainly tell the emperor that the stuff pleases me very much."

"We are delighted to hear you say so," said the swindlers, and then they named all the colors and described the peculiar pattern. The old minister paid great attention to what they said, so as to be able to repeat it when he got home to the emperor.

Then the swindlers went on to demand more money, more silk, and more gold thread, to be able to proceed with the weaving; but they put it all into their own pockets—not a single strand was ever put into the loom, but they went on as before, weaving at the empty loom.

The emperor soon sent another faithful official to see how the stuff was getting on and if it would soon be ready. The same thing happened to him as to the minister; he looked and looked, but as there was only the empty loom, he could see nothing at all.

"Is this not a beautiful piece of stuff?" said both the swindlers, showing and explaining the beautiful pattern and colors which were not there to be seen.

"I know I am not a fool!" thought the man. "So it must be that I am unfit for my good post! It is very strange, though! However, one must not let it appear!" So he praised the stuff he did not see and assured them of his delight in the beautiful colors and the originality of the design. "It is absolutely charming!" he said to the emperor. Everybody in the town was talking about this splendid stuff.

Now the emperor thought he would like to see it while it was still on the loom. So, accompanied by a number of selected courtiers, among whom were the two faithful officials who had already seen the imaginary stuff, he went on to visit the crafty impostors, who were working away as hard as ever they could at the empty loom.

"It is magnificent!" said both the officials. "Only see, Your Majesty, what a design! What colors!" And they pointed to the empty loom, for they thought no doubt the others could see the stuff.

"What!" thought the emperor. "I see nothing at all! This is terrible! Am I a fool? Am I not fit to be emperor? Why, nothing worse could happen to me!"

"Oh, it is beautiful!" said the emperor. "It has my highest approval!" And he nodded his satisfaction as he gazed at the empty loom. Nothing would induce him to say that he could not see anything.

The whole suite gazed and gazed but saw nothing more than all the others. However, they all exclaimed with His Majesty: "It is very beautiful!" and they advised him to wear a suit made of this wonderful cloth on the occasion of a great procession which was just about to take place. "It is magnificent! Georgeous! Excellent!" went from mouth to mouth; they were all equally delighted with it. The emperor gave each of the rogues an order of knighthood to be worn in their buttonholes and the title of "Gentlemen Weavers."

The swindlers sat up the whole night, before the day on which the procession was to take place, burning sixteen candles, so that people might see how anxious they were to get the emperor's new clothes ready. They pretended to take the stuff off the loom. They cut it out in the air with a huge pair of scissors, and they stiched away with needles without any thread in them. At last they said: "Now the emperor's new clothes are ready!"

The emperor, with his grandest courtiers, went to them himself, and both the swindlers raised one arm in the air, as if they were holding something, and said, "See, these are the trousers, this is the coat, here is the mantle!" and so on. "It is as light as a spider's web. One might think one had nothing on, but that is the very beauty of it!"

"Yes!" said all the courtiers, but they could not see anything, for there was nothing to see.

"Will Your Imperial Majesty be graciously pleased to take off your clothes," said the impostors, "so that we may put on the new ones, along here before the great mirror."

The emperor took off all his clothes, and the impostors pretended to give him one article of dress after the other, of the new ones which they had pretended to make. They pretended to fasten something round his waist and to tie on something; this was the train, and the emperor turned round and round in front of the mirror.

"How well His Majesty looks in the new clothes! How becoming they are," cried all the people round. "What a design, and what colors! They are most gorgeous robes!"

"The canopy is waiting outside which is to be carried over Your Majesty in the procession," said the master of ceremonies.

"Well, I am quite ready," said the emperor. "Don't the clothes fit well?" And then he turned around again in front of the mirror, so that he should seem to be looking at his grand things.

The chamberlains who were to carry the train stooped and pretended to lift it from the ground with both hands, and they walked along with their hands in the air. They dared not let it appear that they could not see anything.

Then the emperor walked along in the procession under the gorgeous canopy, and everybody in the streets and at the windows exclaimed, "How beautiful the emperor's new clothes are! What a splendid train! And they fit to perfection!" Nobody would let it appear that he could see nothing, for then he would not be fit for his post, or else he was a fool.

None of the emperor's clothes had been so successful before.

"But he has got nothing on," said a little child.

"Oh, listen to the innocent," said his father, and one person whispered to the other what the child had said. "He has nothing on; a child says he has nothing on!"

"But he has nothing on!" at last cried all the people.

The emperor squirmed for he knew it was true, but he thought, "The procession must go on now," so he held himself stiffer than ever, and the chamberlains held up the invisible train.

The Miller, His Son, and Their Donkey

by Aesop

A miller and his son were driving their donkey to a neighboring fair to sell him. They had not gone far when they met a group of girls returning from town, laughing and talking together.

"Look there!" cried one of them. "Did you ever see such fools, to be trudging along the road on foot, when they ought to be riding!"

So the man put the boy on the donkey, and they went on their way. Presently they came up to a group of old men in earnest debate. "There!" said one of them. "That proves exactly what I was saying. No one pays any respect to old age in these days. Look at that idle young rogue riding, while his poor old father has to walk. Get down, you lazy lout, and let the old man rest his weary limbs."

The miller made his son dismount and got on the donkey's back in his place. And in this manner they proceeded along the way until they met a company of women and children.

"Why, shame on you, lazybones!" they cried. "How can you ride while that poor little lad can hardly keep up with you?" The good miller, wishing to please, took up his son to sit behind him.

But just as they reached the edge of the village a townsman called out to them: "I have a good mind to report you to the authorities for overloading that poor beast so shamelessly. You big hulking fellows should better be able to carry that donkey than the other way round."

So, alighting, the miller and his son tied the beast's legs together and, with a pole across their shoulders, carried the donkey over the bridge that led to the town. This was such an entertaining sight to the townsfolk that crowds came out to laugh at it. The poor animal, frightened by the uproar, began to struggle to free himself. In the midst of the turmoil the donkey slipped off the pole and over the rail of the bridge into the water and was washed away down the river.

Moral: Try to please all and you end by pleasing none.

The Fox and the Grapes

by Aesop

Once there was a hungry fox who saw a bunch of grapes hanging up high from a tall grapevine.

"Oh," said the fox. "I'll bet those grapes are good and sweet."

Then he jumped and jumped, but no matter how hard he tried he couldn't reach the grapes. So the fox left the grapes hanging there and went off muttering, "I'll bet those grapes were sour anyway!"

Moral: Just because you can't have something you want doesn't mean it has turned sour.

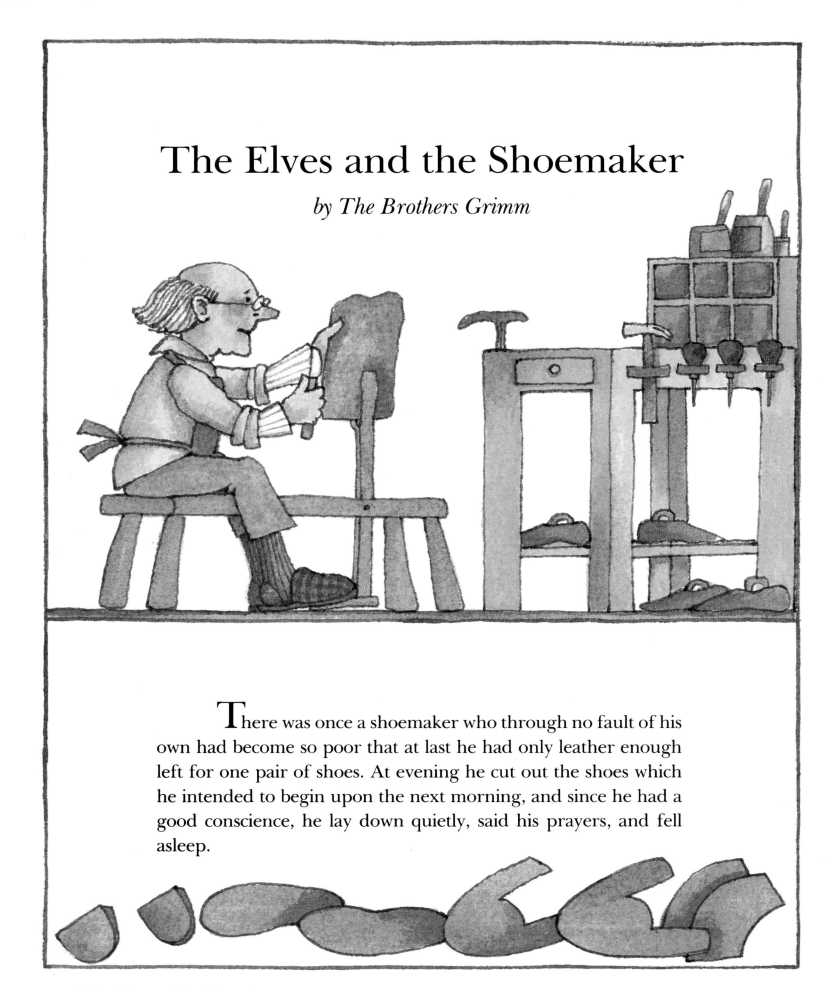

The Elves and the Shoemaker

by The Brothers Grimm

There was once a shoemaker who through no fault of his own had become so poor that at last he had only leather enough left for one pair of shoes. At evening he cut out the shoes which he intended to begin upon the next morning, and since he had a good conscience, he lay down quietly, said his prayers, and fell asleep.

In the morning, when he had said his prayers and was preparing to sit down to work, he found the pair of shoes standing finished on his table. He was amazed and could not understand it in the least.

He took the shoes in his hand to examine them more closely. They were so neatly sewn that not a stitch was out of place, and they were as good as the work of a master hand.

Soon afterwards a customer came in, and as he was much pleased with the shoes, he paid more than the ordinary price for them, so that the shoemaker was able to buy leather for two pairs of shoes with the money.

He cut them out in the evening, and the next day with fresh courage was about to go to work. But he had no need to, for when he got up the shoes were finished, and buyers were not lacking. These gave him so much money that he was able to buy leather for four pairs of shoes.

Early next morning he found the four pairs finished, and so it went on. What he cut out at evening was finished in the morning, so that he was soon again in comfortable circumstances and became a well-to-do man.

Now it happened one evening not long before Christmas, when he had cut out some shoes as usual, that he said to his wife, "How would it be if we were to sit up tonight to see who it is that lends us such a helping hand?"

The wife agreed and lighted a candle, and they hid themselves in the corner of the room behind the clothes which were hanging there. At midnight came two little naked men who sat down at the shoemaker's table, took up the cut-out work, and began with their tiny fingers to stitch, sew, and hammer so neatly and quickly that the shoemaker could not believe his eyes. They did not stop till everything was quite finished and stood complete on the table. Then they ran swiftly away.

The next day the wife said, "The little men have made us rich, and we ought to show our gratitude. They were running about with nothing on, and must freeze with cold. Now I will make them little shirts, coats, waistcoats, and trousers, and will even knit them a pair of stockings. And you shall make them each a pair of gloves."

The husband agreed. And at evening, when they had everything ready, they laid out the presents on the table and hid themselves to see how the little men would behave.

At midnight they came skipping in and were about to set to work. But instead of the leather already cut out, they found the charming little clothes.

At first they were surprised, then delighted. With great speed they put on and smoothed down the pretty clothes, singing:

"Now we're boys so fine and neat,
Why cobble more for others' feet?"

Then they hopped and danced about, and leapt over chairs and tables and out the door. Henceforward they came back no more, but the shoemaker fared well as long as he lived and had good luck in all his undertakings.

Chicken Licken

by P.C. Asbjörnsen

One day when Chicken Licken was scratching among the leaves, an acorn fell out of a tree and struck her on the tail.

"Oh," said Chicken Licken, "the sky is falling! I am going to tell the King."

So she went along and went along until she met Henny Penny.

"Good morning, Chicken Licken, where are you going?" said Henny Penny.

"Oh, Henny Penny, the sky is falling and I am going to tell the King!"

"How do you know the sky is falling?" asked Henny Penny.

"I saw it with my own eyes, I heard it with my own ears, and a piece of it fell on my tail!" said Chicken Licken.

"Then I will go with you," said Henny Penny.

So they went along and went along until they met Cocky Locky.

"Good morning, Henny Penny and Chicken Licken," said Cocky Locky, "where are you going?"

"Oh, Cocky Locky, the sky is falling and we are going to tell the King!"

"How do you know the sky is falling?" asked Cocky Locky.

"Chicken Licken told me," said Henny Penny.

"I saw it with my own eyes, I heard it with my own ears, and a piece of it fell on my tail!" said Chicken Licken.

"Then I will go with you," said Cocky Locky, "and we will tell the King."

So they went along and went along until they met Ducky Daddles.

"Good morning, Cocky Locky, Henny Penny, and Chicken Licken," said Ducky Daddles, "where are you going?"

"Oh Ducky Daddles, the sky is falling and we are going to tell the King!"

"How do you know the sky is falling?" asked Ducky Daddles.

"Henny Penny told me," said Cocky Locky.

"Chicken Licken told me," said Henny Penny.

"I saw it with my own eyes, I heard it with my own ears, and a piece of it fell on my tail!" said Chicken Licken.

"Then I will go with you," said Ducky Daddles, "and we will tell the King."

So they went along and went along until they met Goosey Loosey.

"Good morning, Ducky Daddles, Cocky Locky, Henny Penny, and Chicken Licken," said Goosey Loosey, "where are you going?"

"Oh, Goosey Loosey, the sky is falling and we are going to tell the King!"

"How do you know the sky is falling?" asked Goosey Loosey.

"Cocky Locky told me," said Ducky Daddles.

"Henny Penny told me," said Cocky Locky.

"Chicken Licken told me," said Henny Penny.

"I saw it with my own eyes, I heard it with my own ears, and a piece of it fell on my tail!" said Chicken Licken.

"Then I will go with you," said Goosey Loosey, "and we will tell the King!"

So they went along and went along until they met Turkey Lurkey.

"Good morning, Goosey Loosey, Ducky Daddles, Cocky Locky, Henny Penny, and Chicken Licken," said Turkey Lurkey, "where are you going?"

"Oh, Turkey Lurkey, the sky is falling and we are going to tell the King!"

"How do you know the sky is falling?" asked Turkey Lurkey.

"Ducky Daddles told me," said Goosey Loosey.

"Cocky Locky told me," said Ducky Daddles.

"Henny Penny told me," said Cocky Locky.

"Chicken Licken told me," said Henny Penny.

"I saw it with my own eyes, I heard it with my own ears, and a piece of it fell on my tail!" said Chicken Licken.

"Then I will go with you," said Turkey Lurkey, "and we will tell the King!"

So they went along and went along until they met Foxy Woxy.

"Good morning, Turkey Lurkey, Goosey Loosey, Ducky Daddles, Cocky Locky, Henny Penny, and Chicken Licken," said Foxy Woxy, "Where are you going?"

"Oh, Foxy Woxy, the sky is falling and we are going to tell the King!"

"How do you know the sky is falling?" asked Foxy Woxy.

"Goosey Loosey told me," said Turkey Lurkey.

"Ducky Daddles told me," said Goosey Loosey.

"Cocky Locky told me," said Ducky Daddles.

"Henny Penny told me," said Cocky Locky.

"Chicken Licken told me," said Henny Penny.

"I saw it with my own eyes, I heard it with my own ears, and a piece of it fell on my tail," said Chicken Licken.

"Then we will run, we will run to my den," said Foxy Woxy, "and I will tell the King."

So they all ran to Foxy Woxy's den, and the King was never told that the sky was falling.

The Tortoise and the Hare

by Aesop

Once there was a hare who met a tortoise on the road. "How slow you are," said the hare to the tortoise.

"Not as slow as you might think," said the tortoise. "In fact, I'll challenge you to a race."

"Done," said the hare. *And that will be the easiest race I've ever won,* thought the hare.

They asked the fox to be the judge and started out. In no time at all, the hare was far ahead of the tortoise.

"I am so far ahead that I think I'll just lie down under this tree and take a nap. I'll be able to catch up to the tortoise with no trouble at all!" And the hare lay down and fell asleep.

The tortoise kept going along at a steady pace and soon passed the sleeping hare. In a little while the hare woke and rushed along but the tortoise had already crossed the finish line and won!

Moral: Slow and steady wins the race.

The Cat and the Mouse

by Joseph Jacobs

The cat and the mouse
Play'd in the malt-house:

The cat bit off the mouse's tail. "Pray, Puss, give me my tail." "No," said the cat, "I'll not give you your tail, till you go to the cow, and fetch me some milk."

First she leapt, and then she ran,
Till she came to the cow, and thus began:

"Pray, Cow, give me milk, that I may give Cat milk, that Cat may give me my own tail again." "No," said the cow. "I will give you no milk, till you go to the farmer and get me some hay."

First she leapt, and then she ran,
Till she came to the farmer, and thus began:

"Pray, Farmer, give me hay, that I may give Cow hay, that Cow may give me milk, that I may give Cat milk, that Cat may give me my own tail again." "No," said the farmer, "I'll give you no hay, till you go to the butcher and fetch me some meat."

First she leapt, and then she ran,
Till she came to the butcher, and thus began:

"Pray, Butcher, give me meat, that I may give Farmer meat, that Farmer may give me hay, that I may give Cow hay, that Cow may give me milk, that I may give Cat milk, that Cat may give me my own tail again." "No," said the butcher, "I'll give you no meat, till you go to the baker and fetch me some bread."

First she leapt, and then she ran,
Till she came to the baker, and thus began:

"Pray, Baker, give me bread, that I may give Butcher
bread, that Butcher may give me meat, that I may
give Farmer meat, that Farmer may give me hay, that
I may give Cow hay, that Cow may give me milk, that
I may give Cat milk, that Cat may give me my own tail
again."

"Yes, said the baker, "I'll give you some bread,
But if you eat my meal, I'll cut off your head."

Then the baker gave Mouse bread, and Mouse gave
Butcher bread, and Butcher gave Mouse meat, and
Mouse gave Farmer meat, and Farmer gave Mouse
hay, and Mouse gave Cow hay, and Cow gave Mouse
milk, and Mouse gave Cat milk, and Cat gave
Mouse her own tail again.

The Shepherd Who Cried "Wolf"

by Aesop

Once there was a shepherd boy who watched his flock of sheep in a field just outside the village. There was so little to do one day, he decided to have some fun.

"Help, help!" he cried. "Wolf! Wolf! The wolves are among my lambs."

All the villagers came running, with hoes and pitchforks to save the flock from the wolves. When they got there the shepherd boy laughed and said, "There are no wolves. And did you all look funny running so fast, panting for breath!" The villagers all went back to their houses and their work, not too pleased that the shepherd boy had fooled them.

Twice, three times more, the shepherd boy cried "Wolf! Wolf!" and twice, three times more, the villagers ran to help. The shepherd boy thought this was a great joke!

But, finally the wolves *did* come! And as they began to make off with the sheep the shepherd boy ran crying for help. "You'll not fool us again," the villagers said, and kept at their work and in their homes.

And the poor shepherd boy lost all his flock.

Moral: When people tell lie after lie nobody believes them when they speak the truth.

How Jack Went to Seek His Fortune

by Joseph Jacobs

Once upon a time there was a boy named Jack and one morning he decided to go and seek his fortune.

He hadn't gone very far before he met a cat.

"Where are you going, Jack?" said the cat.

"I am going to seek my fortune."

"May I go with you?"

"Yes," said Jack, "the more the merrier."

So on they went, jiggelty-jolt, jiggelty-jolt.

They went a little farther and they met a dog.

"Where are you going, Jack?" said the dog.

"I am going to seek my fortune."

"May I go with you?"

"Yes," said Jack, "the more the merrier."

So on they went, jiggelty-jolt, jiggelty-jolt.

They went a little farther and they met a goat.
"Where are you going, Jack?" said the goat.
"I am going to seek my fortune."
"May I go with you?"
"Yes," said Jack, "the more the merrier."
So on they went, jiggelty-jolt, jiggelty-jolt.
They went a little farther and they met a bull.
"Where are you going, Jack?" said the bull.
"I am going to seek my fortune."
"May I go with you?"
"Yes," said Jack, "the more the merrier."
So on they went, jiggelty-jolt, jiggelty-jolt.
They went a little farther and they met a rooster.
"Where are you going, Jack?" said the rooster.
"I am going to seek my fortune."
"May I go with you?"
"Yes," said Jack, "the more the merrier."
So on they went, jiggelty-jolt, jiggelty-jolt.

Well, they went on till it was nearly evening, and they began to think of some place where they could spend the night. About this time they came in sight of a house, and Jack told them to keep still while he went up and looked in through the window. And inside there were some robbers counting their money. Then Jack went back and told the animals to wait till he gave the word and then to make all the noise they could. So when they were all ready Jack gave the word, and the cat mewed, and the dog barked, and the goat bleated, and the bull bellowed, and the rooster crowed, and altogether they made such a dreadful noise that it frightened the robbers all away.

And then they went in and took over the house. Jack was afraid the robbers would come back during the night. So when it was time to go to bed he put the cat in the rocking-chair, and he put the dog under the table, and he put the goat upstairs, and he put the bull in the cellar, and the rooster flew up onto the roof, and Jack went to bed.

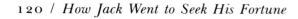

By-and-by the robbers saw it was all dark and they sent one man back to the house to look for their money. Before long he came back in a great fright and told them his story.

"I went back to the house," said he, "and went in and tried to sit down in the rocking-chair, and there was an old woman knitting, and she stuck her knitting-needles into me." That was the cat, you know.

"I went to the table to look for the money, and there was a shoemaker under the table, and he hammered his nails into me." That was the dog, you know.

"I started to go upstairs, and there was a man up there thresh-ing, and he knocked me down with his flail." That was the goat, you know.

"I started to go down to the cellar, and there was a man down there chopping wood, and he knocked me back upstairs with his axe." That was the bull, you know.

"But I wouldn't have minded all that if it hadn't been for that little fellow on top of the house, who kept a-hollering, 'Chuck him up to me-e! Chuck him up to me-e!'" Of course that was the cock-a-doodle-do.

The House on the Hill

by P.C. Asbjörnsen

Once upon a time a curly-tailed pig said to his friend the sheep, "I am tired of living in a pen. I am going to build me a house on the hill."

"Oh! May I go with you?" said the sheep.

"What can you do to help?" asked the pig.

"I can haul the logs for the house," said the sheep.

"Good!" said the pig. "You are just the one I want. You may go with me."

As the pig and the sheep walked and talked about their new house, they met a goose.

"Good morning, Pig," said the goose. "Where are you going this fine morning?"

"We are going to the hill to build us a house. I am tired of living in a pen," said the pig.

"Honk!" said the goose. "May I go with you?"

"What can you do to help?" asked the pig.

"I can gather moss and stuff it into the cracks with my bill to keep out the wind and rain."

"Good!" said the pig and the sheep. "You are just the one we want. You may go with us."

As the pig and the sheep and the goose walked and talked about their new house, they met a rabbit.

"Good morning, Rabbit," said the pig.

"Good morning," said the rabbit. "Where are you going this fine morning?"

"We are going to the hill to build us a house. I am tired of living in a pen," said the pig.

"Oh!" said the rabbit, with a quick little jump. "May I go with you?"

"What can you do to help?" asked the pig.

"I can dig the holes for the posts of your house," said the rabbit.

"Good!" said the pig and the sheep and the goose. "You are just the one we want. You may go with us."

As the pig and the sheep and the goose and the rabbit walked and talked about their new house, they met a cock.

"Good morning, Cock," said the pig.

"Good morning," said the cock. "Where are you going this fine morning?"

"We are going to build us a house. I am tired of living in a pen," said the pig.

The cock flapped his wings three times. "Oh, Oh, Oh, O-O-Oh!" he crowed. "May I go with you?"

"What can you do to help?" asked the pig.

"I can be your clock," said the cock. "I will crow every morning and wake you up at daybreak."

"Good!" said the pig and the sheep and the goose and the rabbit. "You are just the one we want. You may go with us."

Then they all went happily to the hill. The pig found the logs for the house. The sheep hauled them. The rabbit dug the holes for the posts. The goose stuffed moss in the cracks to keep out the rain. And every morning the cock crowed to wake up the workers.

When at last the house was finished, the cock flew to the very top of it, and crowed and crowed and crowed.